D1053168

THE
SCHOOL PLAY
FROM THE
BLACK LAGOON®

THE
SCHOOL PLAY
FROM THE
BLACK LAGOON®

by Mike Thaler
Illustrated by Jared Lee

SCHOLASTIC INC.

New York   Toronto   London   Auckland
Sydney   Mexico City   New Delhi   Hong Kong

To my beautiful wife, Patty, my right hand and all my heart.—M.T.
To classmate Teresa (Nelson) Fratus.—J.L.

visit us at www.abdopublishing.com

Reinforced library bound edition published in 2014 by Spotlight, a division of the ABDO Group, PO Box 398166, Minneapolis, MN 55439. Spotlight produces high-quality reinforced library bound editions for schools and libraries. Published by agreement with Scholastic, Inc.

Printed in the United States of America, North Mankato, Minnesota.
102013
012014
 This book contains at least 10% recycled materials.

Cataloging-in-Publication Data

Thaler, Mike, 1936-
   The school play from the Black Lagoon / by Mike Thaler ; illustrated by Jared Lee.
   p. cm. -- (Black Lagoon adventures; #20)
   Summary: Break a leg? Mrs. Green announces that the class will be putting on a school play. All the kids are excited to audition for "The Legend of Sleepy Hollow" except for Hubie. The only part that he wants is in the audience! But you can't be famous if you never step on stage.
1. Plays--Fiction. 2. Schools--Fiction. 3. Monsters--Fiction. I. Title. II Series.
   PZ7.T3 Scp 2011
   [Fic]--dc23

ISBN 978-1-61479-205-5 (Reinforced Library Bound Edition)

All Spotlight books are reinforced library binding
and manufactured in the United States of America.

CONTENTS

SPRING

SUMMER

FALL

WINTER

6

← YELLOW

CHAPTER 1
THE FALL OF HUBIE

It's the beginning of October, and Mrs. Green announces that our class is going to put on a fall play. Everyone has to try out for it. If I'm picked for a part, it will be my down*fall*.

CROW→

I can't act at all. I'll forget my lines. I'll forget my cues. If I'm lucky—I'll forget to show up.

CHAPTER 2
IT'S CURTAINS

My mom took me to a play once. It was called *Omelet*. It was written by a guy named Will-Ham Shake-A-Spear.

AUTHOR

← EGG

It was about Prince Omelet—he was a good egg. He had a pretty nice mom—the queen—and a really mean stepdad—the step-king. They talked a lot and then everyone started fighting each other with long swords. The play was over when there was no one left except the audience.

CHAPTER 3
STAR TREK

All the other kids are very excited. The play is *The Legend of Sleepy Hollow*. Eric wants to be the star. Penny wants to be the starlet. I just want to be in the audience. It's the safest place. Mrs. Green says tryouts are tomorrow after school. I will *try* to stay *out*.

WOW!

CHAPTER 4
SHOW BUZZ

The school bus is a school buzz. Everyone is excited about the play. I just look out the window. I feel like a leaf. I'll turn red with embarrassment just before I fall.

RED →

MOON →

OTHER THINGS HUBIE
WOULD RATHER DO THAN
BE IN A SCHOOL PLAY

BLAST OFF
TO MARS

PLAY IN THE
WORLD SERIES

RIDE A
DOLPHIN

RUN THE BOSTON
MARATHON

VISIT THE
TITANIC

COOL.

MEET BATMAN

ROBIN →

17

Then I have a daydream. Tomorrow I'll get picked for the leading part. Everyone will want my autograph. I'll go to Hollywood and get a Ferrari. I'll be on the cover of *People* magazine. Hey, this isn't bad after all. It's too bad you can't skip the tryouts and just be a star.

SLEEP → DUST

← HALF ASLEEP (AND HALF AWAKE)

SLEEPING SKULL ↓

CONKED OUT →

SCREAMING FANS →

STAY BACK!

BODYGUARD ←

RED CARPET ↗

SITTING ON A LOS ANGELES PHONE BOOK
↓

FERRARI
↙

PEOPLE
MAGAZINE

HUBIE, A HOT NEW STAR

SOLD OUT IN TEN MINUTES ←

CHAPTER 5
THE PLAY'S THE THING

Mom is excited about the play, too. She says she used to do a little acting. She told me it's fun and she hopes I get a role. I don't want a roll *or* a bagel.

NOTE: MOM SPELLED BACKWARD IS MOM.

NOT A FAMOUS BUG → ... ← JUST ANOTHER BUG

I go to my room. I better practice just in case. I close my door and go to the mirror. I practice expressions: anger, joy, sadness, surprise, fear. Fear comes out the best, because I'm really afraid I'll get a part.

ANGER

JOY

SADNESS

FEAR

SURPRISE

21

CHAPTER 6
STAGE FRIGHT

BURNT OUT

HOME RUN SLUGGER

UNPLUGGED

SCRIPT →

That night I have a dream. I step out onstage. The lights are so bright I can't see the audience, but I hear them breathing. I've got butterflies in my stomach and glue on my tongue. Each foot weighs one thousand pounds and I have to go to the bathroom.

PAPER BUTTERFLY →

Suddenly, I'm in the audience looking up at me on the stage. Everyone begins to boo and throw vegetables. I throw a tomato at myself.

I wake up ducking.

25

CHAPTER 7
HEAD OVER HEALS IN LOVE

The next day on the school bus everyone's still talking about the play.

"I read it last night," says Eric.

"What's it about?" I ask.

"Well, it's sort of a love story," says Eric.

26

"Ick," I say

"But it's more of a ghost story," he quickly adds.

"Great," I say. "Who wrote it?"

"Some guy named Irving Washington."

"Don't you mean Washington Irving?" interrupted Penny.

"Whatever. Anyway, it's about a schoolteacher named Ichabod Crane."

WASHINGTON IRVING →

27

"What subject did he teach?" asks Randy.

"He taught all the subjects—it was a one-room schoolhouse."

"Did it have a cafeteria?" asks Penny.

"I don't think so," says Eric. "It was a long time ago."

"Didn't the kids eat back then?" asks Penny

WATCH OUT!

"They brought their lunches. Anyway, Ichabod *loved* to eat. He would go home with the students whose moms were the best cooks," explains Eric.

"Was he fat?" asks Freddy.

"No, he was very thin. Anyway, one day he was invited over by a very rich farmer who had a beautiful daughter."

"That's the part I'll play!" exclaims Penny.

31

"Where do the ghosts come in?" I ask.

"The story is full of ghosts, but the scariest one is . . ."

"We're here!" shouts T-Rex. "Everybody out!"

LEFTOVER COOTIE
FROM PAGE 18

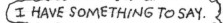
I HAVE SOMETHING TO SAY.

CHAPTER 8
STRAIGHT FROM THE HORSE'S MOUTH

THE LEGEND OF SLEEPY HOLLOW

In the library, Mrs. Beamster tells us the rest of the story.

"In Sleepy Hollow, there were ghosts that haunted every house, every tree, every rock, and every bridge. But the scariest of all was the Headless Horseman."

"Was he part of the Head Start program?" I ask.

I AIN'T GOT NOBODY.

"He was a soldier in the Revolutionary War whose head had been shot off by a cannon-ball. Every night he'd ride out on his big black horse looking for his head."

"How could he look for his head if he didn't have a head?"

"He had a GPS. Anyway, Ichabod believed all the scary stories but he had fallen in love with Katrina, the rich farmer's daughter. So he visited her every day after school to give her singing lessons. But Katrina had a boyfriend, Brom Bones, who quickly became jealous. Brom was a practical joker."

BONES

"I'll play Brom Bones," says Eric.

"You want to play trombones?" I ask.

"You're not funny," growls Eric.

40

"Anyway, one night Ichabod was riding home on his old horse, Gunpowder, when he heard thundering hoofbeats behind him. He looked back and his blood turned cold."

←BUG ☜ ←ROCK WITH EYES

"What did he see?" we all yelled.

Just then the bell rang ending library period. It was time for lunch.

WHAT DID ICHABOD SEE TO TURN HIS BLOOD COLD?

GIANT
SNOWMAN

ESKIMO WARRIORS

POLAR
BEAR

PENGUIN
ZOMBIES

43

(READ PAGE 45 FOR THE ANSWER)

CHAPTER 9
PIE ARE SCARED

There was pumpkin pie for lunch.

"That's what he saw," said Eric, pointing to the pie.

"He saw a piece of pie?" I ask.

"No, he saw a headless rider thundering down on him."

"Was he holding a piece of pie?"

"No, he was holding his head."

"You mean he finally found it?"

"Well, not exactly. It wasn't really his head—it was a pumpkin and it wasn't really a ghost. It was Brom Bones trying to scare his rival away."

"Did it work?"

"It sure did. Brom married Katrina, and Ichabod was never seen around Sleepy Hollow again. Are you going to eat your pie, Hubie?"

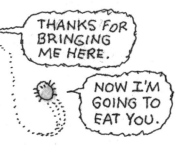

CHAPTER 10
PLAY BALL

Well, it's three o'clock—time for tryouts. All the kids are excited. Mrs. Green is excited. It's the glamour of show biz. I'm not excited. I just want to go home.

SCRIPT →

MEAT LOAF RECIPE →

ZOMBIE

49

"I want to be Brom Bones!" shouts out Eric.

"You got it," says Mrs. Green.

"I want to play Katrina," says Penny, fluttering her eyelashes.

"Oh, no," says Eric.

"You got it," says Mrs. Green.

50

"Okay, but I'm not going to kiss her," insists Eric.

"I'll be Ichabod Crane," says Randy.

"Good choice," says Mrs. Green.

RANDY HUBIE 51

Soon all the parts are gone.

"I'm sorry, Hubie," says Mrs. Green. "You didn't get a part."

"It's okay," I say.

Mrs. Green looks at me.

"Oh, wait a minute," she says. "There's one part left!"

"Wh-what's that?" I stutter.

"The Headless Horseman." Mrs. Green smiles.

CHAPTER 11

RE-HORSING

So I have a part. But it's not so bad. I'm all covered up and have only one line: "Boo!" I can't mess up too badly.

MEMORIZING TIPS

 → BRAIN

1 STUDY YOUR LINES IN A QUIET PLACE, AND NO SNACKS OR PIZZA.

 ↑ YUM

2 WRITE OUT YOUR LINES. THIS WILL HELP YOUR BRAIN COMMIT THEM TO MEMORY. ← PENCIL

3 THINK LIKE THE CHARACTER YOU ARE PLAYING. ← BATMAN

4 BECOME A BROKEN RECORD — SAY LINES OVER AND OVER.

 RECORD ↗

5 STUDY YOUR LINES WHILE MOVING AROUND AS YOU WOULD ONSTAGE.

 ← SCRIPT

6 RECORD YOURSELF SAYING YOUR LINES AND PLAY IT BACK AT BEDTIME.

ON ↓

OFF →

 ↗ TAPE RECORDER

BUG ← ACTOR

When I get home, I go into my room and rehearse my line.

"Boo!"

"BOO!"

"BOOOOO!"

CRYBABY

"Don't cry, Hubie!"

"I'm not crying, Mom. I'm practicing my line."

HUBIE, WHAT'S WRONG?

NOTHING, MOM.

ANXIOUS CROWD →

CHAPTER 12
BLUNDER AND LIGHTNING

← AUDITORIUM

The night of the big play has come. The audience is filing in. They strap a cardboard horse to me and cover me with a black cloth. Then they hand me a jack-o'-lantern. I'm supposed to chase Randy around the stage and throw it at him.

PLAYBILL →

THE LEGEND of SLEEPY HOLLOW

The auditorium lights go out, the stage lights go on, and the curtain goes up. But I can't see too much. At my big moment, they lead me to the stage and push me out. I say, "Boo!" and gallop around the stage. Randy is frightened, and I chase him. He has a head start.

I say, "Boo!" again and throw the pumpkin at him. Randy ducks, and the pumpkin flies out into the audience and hits Mr. Bender, the principal, in the head. The curtain goes down along with Mr. Bender.

CHAPTER 13
ALL'S WELL THAT ENDS WELL

Mr. Bender was a good sport, and we all came out and bowed. Everyone applauded. After the play, Mrs. Green took us out for pizza. Mr. Bender asked me for

STARFISH →

my autograph. Show business is not so bad after all. I might even try out for the play next year. I hope it's *Jaws*. I'd be a great shark.

"TO BE OR NOT TO BE:
THAT IS THE QUESTION"
IS CONSIDERED THE
MOST FAMOUS LINE IN
THEATRE HISTORY.